The Broken Stool and Other Stories

The Broken Stool

& Other Stories

Simon W. Nganga

SPEARS BOOKS
Denver, Colorado

Spears Books
An Imprint of Spears Media Press LLC
7830 W. Alameda Ave, Suite 103-247
Denver, CO 80226
United States of America

First Published in the United States of America in 2024 by Spears Books
www.spearsbooks.org
info@spearsmedia.com
Information on this title: www.spearsbooks.org/the-broken-stool
© 2024 Simon W. Nganga
All rights reserved.

ISBN: 9781957296326 (Paperback)
ISBN: 9781957296333 (eBook)
Also available in Kindle format

Designed and typeset by Spears Media Press LLC
Cover designed by D Kambem

Distributed globally by African Books Collective (ABC)
www.africanbookscollective.com

For my family

Contents

1. To Be Punished When He Next Appears   1

2. The Public Pool   7

3. Everyone Likes Tea   13

4. Ya Bebe   23

5. The Shoelace   33

6. The Broken Stool   42

7. The Swindler   47

8. The Woman Who Never Returned   53

9. Not For Quitters 59

10. Make Masundaaswa   65

Glossary of Terms   71
Acknowledgment   73
About the Author   75

ONE

To Be Punished When He Next Appears

Sifuno grabbed the red pen at the end of the grubby string and swiftly scribbled in the schoolmaster's record book: to be punished when he next appears. His sturdy hands were unsteady, and he was trembling, but he didn't think Chois, his daughter, sitting opposite him on a large administrative table, had noticed.

"Okay. Let's go," his voice was without life, and as Chois rose to leave, her hand knocked over her father's rubber-banded torchphone, and it fell among old books, its parts scattering to different directions. A brief parts-picking contest ensued, and the phone had been reassembled within seconds. She led the way out, avoiding the expression on her father's face.

There was a fresh morning breeze. A rare cold wind hitting his face directly soothed him a little. It was his last trip, so why not make the most of it, he thought. Handing a letter to his errant student, preferring not to say a word to him, Sifuno headed for his old car, his 19-year-old daughter following.

"We'll stop on the escarpment and have coffee together," he sounded remote.

Chois looked at her father for a while. "What's wrong, Sifuno?" She had no problem calling him by name; he preferred it that way.

He thought, trying to read my mind again, trying to appear concerned. Aloud, he said, "I feel dizzy, and I have a throbbing pulse. But this will pass soon."

Chois reached for her ball of wool, took out her unfinished sweater, and busied herself with knitting. When Sifuno braked suddenly and she raised her eyes off her pullover-in-the-making, Sifuno said, "See, you do know how to drive life, don't you?"

Her dark eyes bulged. "Well, you are right. At least you referred me to some books and a few speakers here and there. I've also seen you making attempts at it."

"I had better repeat- just in case I'm away and you must drive yourself to heights."

"Dad, you're kidding, right? Away, away, what do you mean? Of course, you'll be here, there, everywhere for me. Why belabour the point?" her thick lips parted.

"You save five and use five. That's if you earn ten. I must repeat, earn. We lose freedom when we don't earn. Then you can start something, such as a small business, where you can keep busy and earn money. Keep some money somewhere and also venture into something."

"Okay, I get it. But why all these?" Chois ran her

fingers through her hair like one who'd lost something and was desperate. "Sounds obvious. Besides, you have repeated far too many times."

He looked at her. Her dimple, sharp forehead and thick lips were from his mother. Now, they meant nothing. She had tormented him, tightened the belt around his waist, almost cutting it. The failure of daughter's love. He was tired; he longed for a rest to lull his thoughts.

No, that wasn't love. She had pressed him, twisted him, bled him with countless demands. And yet she had defied his word, his command, his advice. And in public, she'd denigrated his little effort, the effort of a schoolmaster.

Now was the day. He'd show her the blisters on his life. Just in a few minutes.

"Just a throbbing pulse and churning stomach, that's all," he said slowly. Then they were on the escarpment. He drove to the side of the road, and they had coffee.

The heat from the midday sun was tempered by a cool wind from the lower ground, where thick lines of smoke billowed out of the charcoal mounds. And when Sifuno saw thick smoke hanging low above them, he said, "When you get to these high places, cover yourself well; this smoky breeze can damage your lungs." His words were drowned by the in-cutting wind. She nodded as she gathered the loose parts of her red sweater.

Sifuno's entire frame was gripped by fear. He had been this way for some time and had learned to place fear in its place. Now, he could suppress no more of it.

It had broken its banks and was soaking his entire self. He was literally chock-full of it.

He knew the case at the forest department had been filed. Those green vehicles at his compound, the officers' questions, and the many policies they'd quoted. True, there had been many charcoal burners, but his case was different. How could he construct a charcoal store at his home? Wasn't he promoting the cutting down of trees? And why had he been so adamant on an issue for which so many things in his compound could be used as evidence?

He had not added the details of the botched tender discussed at the head office, details on how he'd received a million and wired back two hundred thousand to an officer at the head office. Wasn't he a conduit? Wasn't he a terminal of theft at the school level?

In the morning, he would be arrested, of course, and arraigned in court. He would go through a series of long trials in different courts—the usual path for stubborn breakers of the law. He would be sacked and his pension taken. His life was cracking, crumbling, collapsing.

And all this because of Chois. He could deny her nothing: the jewellery, the expensive mobile phones and data bundles with them, evenings out with prospective politicians, trips to Mombasa for this and that. How in God's name did she think he'd paid for these?

He propped himself on a nearby acacia, avoiding its thorny parts. The smell of charcoal scorched his nostrils; there was smoke everywhere. "Let's go up the escarpment," he suggested. He preferred to sit on the back of the old Chevrolet "so that I can look at the blue lowlands for the last time." The last four words were inaudible.

Turning on the engine and engaging the gear noisily, Chois saw her father's reaction in the side mirror. As the pick-up started the ascent, her heart sank. She shouldn't have let him sit there, she thought. But then he was getting older and touchier; she didn't think it necessary to question him further. Hadn't she seen how distant he sounded lately?

She held the steering wheel with both hands and concentrated on avoiding the many stones, holes, and broken sticks that marked the escarpment road.

When he was sure she wasn't looking at the rear-view mirror, he stepped onto the iron bar just above the rear bumper. Holding the rim of the trailer, he crouched so that Chois could not see him. Then, loosening his grip, he lowered himself onto the road and into the mix of smoke, dust, flying sticks, and colliding rocks.

He hung among the branches for some time, and his mind was hazy. He could not tell what time it was and tried to avoid smoke and bright light as much as possible. They brought tears and pain to his eyes. He could no longer hear the engine roaring. He could no longer remember the impact as he touched the jagged road, the rolling and the crashing into the shrubs on the side of the road.

He started to feel cold, and he began to free himself

from the thorny branches. As he fell further through the thickets, he heard sticks breaking. An abrupt awareness of where he was struck him. He saw himself as a bundle of pain in the near-dry prickly thickets.

He then heard the strained roar of engines in a few cars climbing the escarpment. The smell of burning charcoal still permeated the air around him, burning his skin. Above him, a few feathery clouds covering the sun were visible through his half-open eyes. He gasped for breath, looking for where to put his aching right leg. His head was heavy and painful.

The thought that he was going to die and that it had been his choice struck him suddenly. It scared him. He shouted. He shouted again. The foggy air entered his mouth. He coughed. He coughed again.

When he opened his eyes, he saw, through the mist of his pain, the blurred shape of a woman. It was his daughter; she had returned and was bending over him. She dragged him out of the thickets and into the car. He then understood that he was still alive, and he sobbed, "Oh me, oh poor me."

TWO

The Public Pool

Omukhurarwa, Rarua for short, paused at the balcony of room 214 on the second floor of Black End Hotel to absorb and respond to the sizzling heat of the January afternoon. He thought of January - dry, dusty, windy, and probably very indifferent. Too bad.

He looked up and caught her lean figure outside an open door on the first floor of the Elcons, about two hundred meters away. Nekeu raised both her hands and signed that they meet below. She then sauntered along the balcony to the staircase at the Western end of the building.

Immaculate, from brown jeans to a lemon T-shirt and dark glasses, Rarua descended the steps, clutching a red suitcase in his hand. Not a hair out of place or a fold on his T-shirt hinted at his night exploit. His burly shoulders visible through his T-shirt, his eyes behind the glasses were clear and alert.

Two more steps of the spiral staircase and he was standing at the venue and in a quickly growing rowdy crowd in front of a high scorpion-flowered gate. About twenty security officers, instructed to let in only professional swimmers, were trying to keep the crowd away. A stranger had ruffled the peace at the pool the previous night.

As soon as he entered, the stranger made believe he was going to shoot someone at the BC bank, the Easy Go hardware and the Roar-I-Roar-back club, and collecting wads of notes, he'd headed north towards the pool. A guard had reported seeing a leg in a tight blue jeans fly over the fence. On the inside, he'd found no one, caught no one and heard nothing save for the sounds of miniature waves breaking at the foot of the pavilion.

Now, as the melee continued at the gate, word had it that in the pool, the oldest crocodile had been sighted struggling to remove a piece of cloth stuck in its old, brown teeth. "That must be my cousin's," a tender voice cut Rarua's heart like a knife. He looked at the scorpion flowers for a while and then broadened his focus to take in a delicate lip and a chubby cheek on which her left hand rested.

She stood two strides away, jumping perpetually in denial. Beautiful, chocolate, slender and thoroughly anxious. She said again, "Oh heavens let it not be him." "Oh no, what again you poor thing," Rarua's legs weakened. From the corner of his eye he saw that she'd seen him. Then in a split second he was in her soft warm arms.

"Please don't let my cousin go," she muttered amidst uncontrollable sobs.

"We have been through this," he raised his voice above the din. Now agitated men and women like soda bottles on transit were jumping up and down, their voices uneven, their sweaty bodies touching and parting unconventionally, and their heads shiny in the midday sun. "And we made it together," she cried from just under his chin, tears from her left eye already wetting his left breast.

That was about five years ago today. The Elcons had not been built, and the pool was unfenced. They'd come to see - perhaps - the oldest croc on the continent, fed, taken care of and named by settlers and now by the villagers. "He'd tried to swim when the croc cut his leg," she tightened her grip. "But that was then. That was understandable. But now…why would one da…" his throat dried up suddenly. Omukhurarwa tried to free himself.

She lifted her head off his chest to look directly into his eyes. She was 25, hailed from Western and danced like Madillu. Yes, she'd be glad to have dinner with him that night. She'd been at the Elcons only for three days and had not met anybody who was fun to be with. "We've only met in crisis days," he felt her grip loosen. "I hate it that we met this one time, too," she stood back and gave him a final pleading look.

Already, the security guards were removing the chain from the gate. He took the card from his wallet, showed it to the guards, and walked into the pool, leaving his red briefcase in Nekeu's care. Just as one guard, pushed hard by the crowd trying to follow Rarua into the pool, fell on an out-of-form bicycle adorned with flags from countries all over the world, he struggled to get on his feet. His colleagues pushed the crowd back and closed the gate.

Rarua's first impression when he entered the pool was of a deserted, rich place. His eyes went round. The rim of the pool: bushy and dusty and rocky in some places; the parlour with terraces: perhaps something for the politician; the water: greening and shiny and scary. Her cousin was somewhere in the ominous water, inhabited by things that had no idea about belonging. He'd finish this task in a few hours. At least he was doing it during the day.

He smiled at the thought that he'd made some arrangements before dinner. For instance, he'd paid two thousand shillings to reserve a table at the Elcons, a place for the chosen few. He'd received a call from the city, and he'd instructed the caller to keep his head. Yes, 100 million was a good price, but then things had changed; the pool had been fenced, security guards engaged, and villagers simply shut out.

On the mabati wall, he saw a notch and a crease in the iron sheets. His eyes were afire, and his spine shrunk. He was surprised he'd used the same spot twice, dodging his pursuers. The guards could not recognise him. Had they known, they'd have shut him out or even arrested him. Now, adjusting his jeans by the waist, he walked slowly towards the area of the struggle in the pool.

Like a root stuck in the crevice of a precious stone, an old pair of jeans – canvas-like and frayed in many places - had been rolled in mud, dipped in water; it had been twisted, turned and squeezed. He saw that the reptile had a familiar mark on the side. His heart warmed, sending ripples of strength into muscular hands. His fingers itched. Startled, the oldest often-spoken-about croc swam away.

In a telephone call, he recalled that Nekeu – that astute former housemaid and now a member of the first lady council – had mentioned this particular croc. She had made it clear that she wasn't going for anything less. "Among these transient things, my wide nostrils can smell worth in things." And she was right, as he'd seen a gold chain around her neck; she wore a brown meet-my-wife suit, a shiny member's badge hanging delicately upon it. "Fleeting as we are, we have to exit honourably," she'd told him as she hung up. Rarua shook his head off the reverie. It contains things that weaken men, he thought.

Now, he had to conceal himself and his shadow behind a rock that had been dragged to the pool by settler Tofit for crocs to sun. He'd wait until the crocs reappear before he'd launch his attack. His initial plan was to wrench the trouser from its teeth and to present it as evidence. It is needless to enter the pool, he thought, when a piece of cloth shows the hole its wearer had entered. He'd picked a piece of rock with which he'd try to break the croc's teeth so that his next visit to the pool would be to pick his gem with ease.

Then, a cool wind cut in, and an ominous wave broke on the eastern end of the pool. It was time to go. It was a moment of attack. That was his time. Many things raced in his mind: his two-year-old child with a genetic illness, his mother's debt of a fine village house, his hustling elementary school friends…. But above all, his resolve was clear as the sun. His faith having leapt, he threw his body over the rock and onto the relic.

Rarua lay on the rock, his entire body shaking. He couldn't remember how long his experience with the alligator had been. His trembling fingers tightened around a piece of jeans—his evidence. His hair was brown, and his T-shirt was something between yellow and black. He realised that his jeans were gone.

A mixture of fear and joy hit the guards and a few people at the gate, and as they took flight, they were awed by the strength of one who'd been considered dead, who'd entered the pool and came out two days later naked from the waist down. Rarua gathered his tattered resolve and walked towards the Black End. They'd closed early enough to stop the madman sighted at the pool. His briefcase had enough money. He'd cloth himself and meet Nekeu later at dinner. At the reception, three armed police officers had been dispatched to meet the apparition. On the list of occupants, no name such as Nekeu was found.

THREE

Everyone Likes Tea

When I finished primary school and was due to begin high school, my elder brother scraped a job at the Tekins, and we moved to Litake. Everyone in town came to know him in a matter of weeks because he had been distributing tea. Lexis often told me that he'd landed the best job and that his clients were city people with money they had no use for. He would labour to add that they'd pay and flash the best holiday offers before his eyes for him to choose because he knew when, where and how to serve tea.

The other tea boys were envious of Lexis because their customers were local farmers who knew nothing about money. They'd pay very little, stagger the sum across several months or even just turn arrogant and refuse to pay. Some farmers with accumulated debts would point at the old machines and ask the boys to find willing buyers, sell, and pay themselves.

Yes, Lexis had found a good job. He knew his clients – the pot-bellied men with trousers that got trapped between their legs. He knew their business names, mostly from their smile during tea taking. He knew Grinface; he knew Spring. He could go to their houses or meet them at the pub. He knew how to deliver tea, watch them take and note their reaction. He could attend the exhibitions and evening parties free of charge. They did not run him out or embarrass him before their guests.

The Chetotos of my town were careful whom they allowed in their network. A formidable group of like-minded workers with a watertight welfare, the Chetoto network was one of positions and rewards. Prominent positions in authority and institutions had been earmarked, and recruitment procedures were tailored to the needs of the members and their families. Like a giant bird of prey, the team hovered over the small town and ringed opportunities, cutting out non-members. *Kisilili* is what we call them in our town. It means a scavenger bird with a powerful sight and a terrific scratching and tearing ability. These Kisililis were in all places in town, surveying narrow alleys, dark dungeons, upmarket places…scouting, scouting, scouting. Those who proffered places took a cup of tea to moisten, warm and expand their guts. No one knew where they came from or when they'd leave. We endured them.

When Saturday came, like swarms of blue flies, Kisililis fell upon the town and took over its brew points. After working hard in balconies, rooftops, basements, and town dumps the whole week, they'd go to the town-pulse, their wives and children following. Their wives would fill the malls for a trendy hairdo and a flashy shopping spree. Their wives would line up delicately in front of supermarkets for pedicure and manicure. The young ones would go to the town gym or movie shops. A few farmers would come to the town too and picking the accent, they would go to these joints, not knowing they'd be denied entry. The staff at the drink points would be careful not to let farmers with their rough hands, dirty fingernails, shabby clothes and reckless manners come into their shops. They knew that their customers - needing space to receive and take their tea - would get mad.

"It's these lazy pretenders again," the Chetotos would say. The Chetotos were uneasy seeing so many farmers in dirty gumboots and soiled aprons in town. The farmers' presence made the town look aloof, slow and sleepy.

"Run them out and let the town wake up," they'd tell the staff at the quench points, mostly young ladies selected from the stock of the light-skinned.

The Chetotos were fond of Lexis and not just because of his name, which to them came close to a familiar car brand. They sent him with his tea to be served in a set of cups made and branded in notable foreign countries. Then, they allowed him to dance to their music, listen to their talk and speak to their women because, though he was the son of a farmer, he belonged to the Chetotos. For Lexis, there was nothing to add to their argument. He knew that for many years, farmers – facing the worst effects of the free-market economy – had fetched the least from their corn sales. He thought that if they went to the pubs, they'd spend the little they had on tea, and they'd spare nothing for their families.

At the start of the selection process, my brother pushed me to go to the town beat points to dance to the latest music for free. "Aidono, when do you plan to visit these places for a body shake," he asked.

"At the Neka's home, they'll soon celebrate the birth of a child. There, I will do a body-shake."

"Ooh, Aidono, my brother, please cut it there. At Neka's you will find good music, I agree. And our friends will certainly be there. But see, don't you want to get selected to a good school? You should take tea with people. Aidono, last-born brother, grow up."

"Okay, but I don't want to go there."

"Why?" Lexis' face showed lines of disappointment.

"The Chetotos will think I am a farmer and shout at me."

"No, not at all. Chetotos are generous as they are kind. Besides, most of them are parents of children your age. They surely cannot just throw you out."

For some days, I thought about what my brother had told me, and my mind tossed images of clean, well-built schools where no one failed. I dreamt of having been admitted to a school where young people were being prepared to lead. I saw myself as one of those leaders who appeared on television screens dancing on the dais as crowds cheered wildly.

I spoke to Wafu, a *boda boda* rider from our village. I alighted at the town-clock roundabout. Across the road was the Spindly, my rest point of interest. I crossed the road at the speed of town people. I entered the Spindly, nodding at the two young ladies at the door, and to every question I answered, "yaa". Lexis had not forgotten to advise me that such a response was more acceptable in town. As I walked into the lounge, the plump men in dark suits and clean hands were talking loudly and clapping their hands. Suddenly, they started to whisper. After some countable minutes, they burst out laughing as they clapped and threw their limps youthfully.

The light from numerous bulbs in the ceiling made the white of the high walls and the cream of the sofa intimidating. And the giant fan in the middle of the ceiling worked menacingly. I stood in the middle of the room. I wasn't sure what would happen if I sat on the sofas. I decided I'd wait to be directed. Wasn't I one of the Chetotos?

No one came. One of the Chetotos rose and walked to the counter. I saw a small human head appear on the other side. They talked for a while, the small-headed man nodding. When the fat man returned to the pack, the small-headed man emerged from a small door below the counter and walked in my direction. I was happy. I knew I would be shown where to sit and even be given the programme for the evening.

Though the hotel was open to the public, he explained, people of my kind were not permitted to come.

As he talked, I tried to look straight into his eyes, but my nostrils started to water. I fumbled through my pockets for my handkerchief. I sniffed, sneezed and then looked down. I was in *okala*, shoes made out of old vehicle tyres.

He put his hand on my shoulder and gently swung me round. At the door, he took out a miniature notebook, wrote something and thrust it into my left hand. "There's where you'll take tea and go home before the sun sets," he spoke slowly and with a gentle smiling face.

I struggled to keep back tears as I crossed the road. I thought about many things. There were now so many Chetotos drawn from the school managers, ministry officials and private businesses. They decided what was right and what was wrong. Their word was final. No one would listen to the one who confronted the Chetotos. But, I did not see myself as one of those farmers. I was different. I was young and had passed my exams. Soon, I'd be in college pursuing a career of my choice. Then, a few years later, I'd get a job in a big institution, join the Chetotos, and perhaps even become their leader. Then I recalled what my brother had once told me about the farmers and why the Chetotos always chased them from those hotels. I found it difficult to understand why a farmer would only be allowed into the hotels when the Chetotos were absent.

I unfolded the paper and saw that he'd written Gange and some more details that looked like a name to some unfamiliar street.

"This is behind the town garage," the man adjusting

the time on his wristwatch by looking at the town clock informed me.

An alley made thinner by broken glass, rotting sticks, scrap metal and occasional miniature pools of urine led me to the place. Gange was behind the Simpsons, a garage sold to the town dwellers shortly before independence.

The smell of fried chicken, sounds of colliding metal and shouting men and women making orders confronted me at the Gange. Bobbing up and down as bubbles from boiling porridge, sweaty heads glistened in the three o'clock sun. As if it was a work requirement for the mechanic, each man had his greasy blue aprons buttoned to the waist, leaving a hairy chest open. Tacked into the belt were spanners, pliers, small hammers and screws. Men had their hands in the air to receive their orders, and women thrust a full plate into every upraised hand. Men jostled and cursed, and women served and scolded. Having survived the threat from hot soup on plates flying above, a recent receiver broke out of the pile made cohesive by the need to be served first, and then, like air running into a vacuum, men reassembled viciously.

I stood a few paces away, ensuring I was far enough to be safe. "You can also be served," said a broad-chested man. "I can make an order for you and bring it right here. You don't have to jostle. In return, I only need a cup of tea." That word tea struck my ears like a bell on the schoolyard announcing the punishment hour. Like debris from a rejected construction, thoughts overwhelmed my mind. Here was someone doing what I so badly desired to do. It was true that here, no one cared about looks. Here, there were no narrow-headed and pot-bellied men. In fact, the only person who'd spoken to me had extended his hand to welcome me to do something my brother so joyously did. But I felt repulsed by the smell, the din, the struggle over food, the jostling. I thought I was different. I longed for a world where looks did not matter and one did not need to push around or belong to some group of people to get even a cup of tea.

It was getting late. I walked back to the town clock and found Wafu waiting. We'd agreed to meet by quarter past five. I would then give him a plan of my evening events.

Well, I had no plans, and he did not ask when I climbed his motorbike. As the creaky bike rattled between my legs, I felt strange and lost.

The school opening date was approaching. My brother was leaving for one of his special mysterious trips to the coast. His travel and accommodation had been booked. What was left was for him to board and lodge. I asked him if he was still going to serve tea on the trip. His answer was as slippery as money. I understood.

"What about the local tea errands?" I asked.

He gave me a long side look and said, "Wafu will".

"But eeeh," I pleaded, my voice getting shrill, "why give this chance to Wafu. Am I not your brother?"

Lexis paced to the village well, a stone's throw away.

At the edge of the well he turned to explain something to me.

"Aidono, this thing is not for everyone's ears." He stopped talking. I walked to where he stood. "It is not just about tea. It is also about who you are and what you stand for." As he spoke, veins lined his temples and his eyes narrowed.

"But, how now, my brother? Why? I can understand. Just explain." I had come very close to him. The smell of something decaying hit my nostrils.

"You know" - he stopped to look at a man walking while leaning to one side as one struggling to carry a heavy head. "Whatever it is, let your brother do it," the struggling man blurted.

And so my brother let me.

The evening before the announcement of the selection results was my first day at work. I was excited because my new boss, Mr Grin had promised to introduce me to the Chetotos and to give me a ride through the town. He had also promised to offer tea for my admission to a big school in the City. So, as I sat on his sofa, which was so large to accommodate three grown-ups, he handed me a thick envelope with many writings on it. From a quick look, one could guess that it had been used for over fifteen errands.

"And remember to bring back the teacup," Mr Grin's voice was hard and chilling.

"Yaa," I struggled to speak like a real Chetoto.

"Take it to Mr Spring," he motioned to his desk,

his other words disappearing into a mutter. I could only catch the last two words: "his tea."

I left the room wondering whether he'd forgotten to tell me more. Was I perhaps required to buy the cups myself? But where was tea? Many ideas crossed my mind as I quickened my pace around the tall buildings and into alleys. It was getting dark, and in front of most wealth-points, neon lights were inviting. I had to be fast. I felt insecure in these darkening places. In the lounge at the Spindly, the light was dim and in a corner sat a man who introduced himself as Mr Spring.

"Do you have tea for me?" his grin was bizarrely broad.

I was silent. He snatched the envelope from my hands and said, "Yeah, this tea. Tell him it's done. You go to the city for school tomorrow."

As he lifted his trousers, I saw that he had on the *FAS*, a pair of socks given to farmers by our local farmers' association. As he stuffed the envelope in the FAS, I retraced my young steps through the town, questions preying on my mind.

"Did you remember to bring the teacup?" Mr Grin shouted his question even before I could enter. At the door, farmers were being turned away. Behind me, darkness had drowned all the alleys to the Spindly.

FOUR

Ya Bebe

Frightened, and cold to her spine, Lubale stood behind the door on a weather-beaten wall of her Masanja hut with her right hand on her husband's war spear. Behind her were three drumsticks cut from hardwood, and on the wooden three-legged stool was a hoe she'd been given as a gift on her wedding day.

Facing the tumbledown hut was a giant python, its head resting on the main branch of a shade tree under which Lubale often lay, surveying the leaves and enjoying the cool breeze on sunny days. Its tail was three metres away, coiled upon a tuft of grass. The snake lying there in colossal coils was *ya Bebe*.

Beside Lubale was a cow skin—her bedding—rolled up and made to lean on the banana-leaf wall. Next to it was a double-mouthed water pot with cool water for her husband.

The serpent lay upon the smooth branches of the

shade tree in silence. The wide glassy eyes on the sides of its flat head blazed in response to the sound of the wind, drunkenly rustling through the dry banana leaves. Its eyes strayed to the cow tethered on a tight rope near the barn and back to the round hut.

Five times the creature had encroached upon this lonely hut, and five times it had found no one at home. In all, Lubale had locked herself in the hut three times. She had been chased two times, and her left leg broke once when she sped into the hut, her hideout. The giant snake had perhaps come to see for itself and perhaps to pry behind the delicate door to see what nectar lay so naively yet powerfully behind it. Nothing gave an indication of a human being behind the closed door. Nothing revealed the young woman, barely 16 years old, shaking and sweating behind the newly-made door.

This was the same snake that had molested, out-spied and decimated the young men of the village. It had attacked human dwellings, flushed out and squeezed blood out of young men. It was the snake that seemed to enjoy the ineffective parries from terror-stricken women who - sprinting backwards - stumbled on stones and undergrowths and fell, covering their eyes with their hands as if afraid of seeing the serpent's last action.

Yet, a lone recently married man with a hunch for hunting and a talent at combat had fought it off. He was a mere youth, just at the age of initiation, one who might have married early to fend off pangs of loneliness, and not because he knew what he wanted to do with a woman. He had fought it and made it slither away. Now he was ready to challenge it at the entry to the cave. He was determined to tear his way into the cave through the massive coils.

A glint of trepidation in the serpent's eyes was drowned by the rapid flicker of the thorn-like tongue. Its head rose and fell in the blind brandishing. It was as if it was asking to be shown the defence line, the one that would engage it and be its equal in a fight. Or had it come to test the strength of the narrow door behind which she stood? It was as if it was gloating over the inhabitant of this derelict hut lined with newness and unpolished attraction. It had perhaps come for her as a befitting mockery of its most respected, most talked-about, most experienced attacker, she thought. She stood there, blood drumming in her ears. Her husband had gone to the cave to hunt this very serpent, and she didn't know whether taking advantage of its absence, he'd entered the cave or not. She wanted him to enter and be at peace with himself.

Switching the weight of her body to her left leg, she kept her gaze on this intruder. From the chinks of the wall, she could see its inquisitive eyes searching the length of the breath of her hut. Fearing that it could attack any minute, she muttered a few words of prayer for her husband and wished he could appear. A steady wind cut through the irregular gaps producing a miniature whistle. She prayed that the monster wouldn't interpret this as a signal to attack.

The smell of sweat from her armpits made her sick. This was also her bathing hour, as the sun was overhead and the day humid. But nothing could make her move. Not even the cat-like rat that had left its hideout and was now nibbling at the sole of her foot. She parted her legs, raised the left leg and returned it to the ground with a force that could have crushed the snail's shell. Her assailant had left and was headed for her grain pot. A whistle escaped through her lips, causing the serpent to turn and raise its head in angry anticipation. The branch on which it hung gave in and the serpent lowered its head to the ground and slid away noisily.

The hunting ground was far away to the West, but the famous cave was less than three kilometres to the East. It was there that Mango trekked for fresh supplies of honey and antelope meat. Mango had scoured the hills, but not the cave. Ya Bebe prevented him.

Mango had his drink of milk – his first since sunrise. As his stomach roared in appreciation, he peered through the giant branches of the many trees and shrubs that bearded the upper lip of the cave. From here he could see the happenings at the cave mouth. He could see the outline of the cave: its roof was populated by numerous bats; a stone, like a tongue, seemed to float on the waters of the seasonal river at the floor of the cave. For a moment, the sight of a seasonal river at the floor of the cave snaking its way to the south clouded his mind with worry. He thought of his mother, living all alone at Silitanyi and his wife, young and defenceless at their home. It was not in him to worry for long. He had always felt this urgent obligation to save himself and his village from Ya Bebe's threat. This had started as an idea. Now it was an obsession. Not that he had been asked to do so. He just liked to try things for his mother, and now for his wife.

Suddenly, a piece of dry wood cracked, and Mango turned. Branches swayed vigorously as if caught in the eye of an unusual storm. In a moment, everything seemed to move drunkenly, including the tree upon which he sat. He hugged the stock firmly till he could hear his heart thumping frantically against the rough of the back. He had been in this before. He had seen it all. On one occasion he had fainted when he was hit by dry branches breaking just above his head. Luckily he didn't fall.

He fixed his gaze on the hole that was the famous cave, unexplored by any human being. He wanted to know what lay inside it, to explore its inside and taste the honey. At least, broken combs in the slimy water of the seasonal river at the floor of the cave were enough evidence.

As the noise calmed, he saw Ya Bebe in massive coils at the cave-mouth. He could see the new look of the cave; the upraised head of the snake just near the roof of the cave; the ridge-like folds of the giant snake that ran all the way to the floor of the cave, where a seasonal river chuckled; the tiny hole in the giant loop of an odd snake. A look at its skin from a distance, one would say it had just emerged from an oil pot. Its skin reflected invitingly. Mango's eyes swept his immediate surroundings. He had his spear and arrows. The bow was strapped across his shoulders. His headgear was in place. It was his shield in case the serpent aimed its fangs upon it. His cracked feet were painful but free. He only had a piece of skin strapped around his waist.

Ya Bebe did not notice Mango watching from high up the trees. It had lowered its head and tacked it under the coils. On the floor of the cave, the froth on the slimy water of the seasonal river danced gaily in the afternoon breeze. Ya Bebe did not also notice Mango gently scaling the tree down to the cave mouth. He was sure it had swallowed something that would soon disable its sudden lunges and massive squeezing moves.

He was wrong. The sound from the breaking pieces of wood was, for the serpent, a statement of attack. And attack it did. Mango's left foot had hardly touched the rock on the roof of the cave when he was swept by a tail in flight. He fell into the slimy water of the seasonal river below. As he struggled to gain composure in order to see his enemy, he received a whack of the tail that drove him deeper into the slime. His head drummed with pain, and slime entered his mouth. Defiant, he raised and threw his head backwards in a summersault, avoiding the speedy charge from the serpent. He fell among the rocks about five metres away. The serpent went back to its place and waited.

Mango did not retaliate. He was wet from head to toe. The piece of skin around his waist had been ripped, and his headgear was floating in the water. He picked it up, swinging it to free it from the slime. He walked through the rocks to the west, heading to his wife.

For more than five months, whenever he could venture out, Mango circled the cave, trying to find the best angle of attack. The upper part of the cave was covered by a thick bush made up of thorns and climbers and - where there were no trees - loose stones. All these combined to make this spot non-strategic for a fight that required unrelenting swiftness. On the sides of the cave, the ground took a steep dive, making any ventures impossible. The Western side would have been ideal, but the recent rains had broadened the seasonal river making its water dirty and its course needlessly boggy.

The terrain was not going to smother his resolve. He walked around the cave, skirting the thorny bushes and undergrowth. He carefully examined every piece of wood or rock, weighing, assessing and gauging its utility. His mission was singular and so he chose to bait the snake.

South he went, pushing aside undergrowth, overhanging branches, and climbers. It was furnace-hot, and his skin started to itch. He walked South to the trap he'd set on a rock covered by grass. A female hare was in the trap—still alive and kicking. He set it free and headed with it for the cave.

From the upper part of the cave, having knocked the bait unconscious, Mango threw it such that it fell right in front of the serpent. The serpent did not seek to establish the source. It simply took the bait into its folds and waited.

Lean and red-eyed, Mango kept his determination high. On stone or on a tree he spied the hole. He hoped that the need for food or a desire to hunt might cause Ya Bebe to leave the hole. He waited and hoped for such a slight chance. He hoped that one day he might catch his target asleep and slit its throat. But every time he threw a stick or rock the quick movement of his enemy was sign enough that it was on guard.

He replaced the skin around his waist and repaired his torn headgear. Mosquito bites added swellings upon his skin; they itched and became sores. He'd resolved to kill it inside the cave before returning to his wife. At night, he slept on trees, and during the day, he sunned himself on rocks as he scouted the cave, the trails, and the vantage points. Three times, he saw Ya Bebe move; three times, he saw it return to its place, his bait carefully tacked in its coils.

Once he saw it lower its head to the water below, its tail flapping. Bees came out of the cave and buzzed about it. He hoped they could attack and perhaps kill it. He tiptoed to a position on the rock from where he could watch the combat among creatures in nature. There seemed to be an amicable co-existence between them, and he lay on the rock as the serpent returned to its position.

The lonely youth who fought so desperately and kept the snake at the cave soon became an item of gossip among the girls. At the river points while bathing or at the fireside while cooking, they discussed the young man who seemed to be making no progress in his attempt to kill the snake and enter the cave. Wondering whether he was too young for the task, they marvelled at his determination but feared that he might harm himself in the long run. It was clear to the girls that he was after something which was beyond them.

He walked around the cave, sharpening his knife on stones. Learner every minute, he studied the behaviour of the serpent.

Weary from sleep and out of tactic, Mango walked down from a rock to the cave mouth, a double-edged knife with a thorn-like tip in hand. He cleared some undergrowth and was undeterred by the serpent's steady rise. He matched on, his eye upon the target, his grip tighter upon the knife. His steps were unsteady, but his aim was straight. The serpent's body tightened, and its head rose. The shaking ground, the flowing water, and the swaying trees did not stop him. He flung himself upon the creature, his knife swinging wildly. In a moment, he was in a flood of activity. The fangs stuck in his waxed head gear, he was tossed this way and that. He thrown into the water and flung upon rocks. His knife was with him. Then, in that dreamlike state, the strength in the coils slowly disappeared. As he entered the cave, only its tail twitched.

When Mango came out of the cave, his wife was there to receive him. His headgear was gone. The skin around his waist was shredded, and his aching body was dripping with a mixture of blood, water, and slime. With a stone, she made him a man.

FIVE

The Shoelace

Checking among the night workers, I saw Simbauni was among them again, and Noma, the groundsman, must have seen my enlarged eyes. "That's the third day this week," Proto, the day supervisor, quipped. "He worked day and night yesterday and the day before yesterday. Which makes," he counted with his fingers, "forty-eight hours in all—in three days." I checked.

"Forty-eight hours? At 20 shillings per hour? He must be kidding."

Noma nodded. "He doesn't look that industrious, does he? Or that type."

Standing there in my blue weather-beaten oversized apron, I knew just what Noma meant. Simbauni wasn't the long-range type. He wasn't even one who could face himself whenever work no longer produced adequate wages. He had been working for only two hours, he'd told me once, and knew how to survive on little sleep and more work. In the youth days, he'd been one of those people you would feel honoured to associate with.

Looking at him now, you felt that must have been many years ago. He was of indeterminate age, at a guess, maybe fifty-eight, though it may be much more. His onion-shaped cheeks had lost much colour, but above them, his eyes were keen and interestingly wistful. His body oddly heavy, he appeared like one that could have been easily forgotten. On the farm, he worked like one who could never return, his athletic muscles telling a story of strain, pain and abandon. Every member of our team would have made it, but Mr. Simbauni? I couldn't imagine him working for a day, let alone three days nonstop.

"Wonder what he gets out of this?" I spoke over it for what might have been the fiftieth or so time. "He is the type who would be happier at home enjoying the company of his fifth wife."

"Maybe he hasn't any wife," Noma spoke, "and maybe it's just nostalgia for those good old days when he spent his youthful energy on some far-seeing girls."

That, of course, was the only explanation I thought of as I walked out to the store to collect a few weapons. I spotted Simbauni bending over, folding his trousers and slipping his legs into his freckled boots with a char-acteristic grimace. He stuffed the loose end of his frayed shirt into his trousers and motioned towards me at the speed of one who was careful not to lose something.

Fisi was the team leader escorting us to our place of

work that evening. As he passed me, he nodded slightly in Simbauni's direction. "Well, at least we'll hear, 'You don't know the world,'" he laughed. "Our man has come again."

I nodded back. That was another thing about Simbauni. He was and still is one person who could effortlessly carry you down the lone paths of his chequered life, where you felt something cold pass through your body as you attempted to scale the sharp, slimy walls from where you saw a steaming river below beckoning. When he finished, his eyes were wet, and he saw that we were quiet; he started again, "You don't know the world; I take it all in a stride." He would reassure us as the sun appeared on the horizon.

On the eclipse night, he'd shown us a dark, shiny spot on his left bicep. "You don't know the world; a leader was visiting, and we were waiting," he started. He'd taken a front position and could not budge. Seeing a crowd of men, the leader came and hurled new notes at them. Simbauni could never forget. He was the tallest of the pack. His large hands caught the bundle as numerous hands roughed, squeezed and tore into his body. When he came to, he was alone by the roadside. He later learnt from a friend that the crowd had seen his torn trousers and had stalked away in a huff, "You don't know the world." The bundle was in his crotch, but ambitious nails had cut into his biceps, badly injuring it.

"How does he know the magic of stories and time," I quipped once, playfully. Fisi smiled up from his four feet, showing his broken teeth, and said: "Nothing about knowledge! Just like stories are hideouts. Haven't you noticed things about him in them?"

Remembering that, we winked at each other as we proceeded to open the gate. We boarded the pick-up, and Simbauni sat in the front seat. Usually, I was the only one permitted to sit there, but "he needs a warm place," Fisi agreed hesitantly.

The silence in the cabin of our pick-up was infectious. We listened to the wind as it sped past menacingly, and the jumps we experienced when covering the last two kilometres to the farm "are like those of a man on a horse," I shouted above the din. No one laughed.

Simbauni came out first, holding his trousers with his left hand, his stomach hanging loosely upon his body. I jumped from the back of the pick-up and led the way to the farm. It was approaching seven in the evening, and our out-of-the-way path to the dam had lost its outline. Twice, I stepped on the thick grass that fringed it, stumbled, and regained my balance by holding onto the overhanging foliage.

It had rained heavily two days ago, and the mud submissively grabbed the soles of our rough boots. I let Fisi get to the front while I stayed back to escort Simbauni. "I've fixed this button three times today; you don't know the world." He fished an old shoelace from his pocket and cautiously belted his trousers like one tethering a feral goat.

At last, we were at the hide, inside a temporary

enclosure and out of harm's way. The fireplace was cold, and so were the few pieces of wood, the remains of yesterday's watch-out. Crickets dialogued in turns, and the fireflies dimly lit our place. "You don't know the world," Simbauni started, "we need a fire." We laughed. He struck the matchstick, and I saw that a new snake-like pipe had been dragged toward the thorn fence, one of our uncanny walls.

We had our packed snacks, and then all our men secured their places. The trouble was that evening, Simbauni did not tell his usual stories, and he responded to every pestering in a near rude tone. No more was heard about investing in bets. Ten thirty came, and even the crickets and the fireflies gave up their activities, and so did our men.

"Aaaay," echoed a strange accent from somewhere behind the boys sleeping on empty maize bags about two hours later. "Something has jerked; didn't you say we report every movement?" Fisi was up, his fright-filled eyes glistening in the dimly lit hide-out. No one moved, and the father of three went back to sleep, clicking.

The nippy effect of Simbauni's encounter with stray dogs on his way home after watching a football match, came back, dusting away all the vestiges of courage, and I began to realise that there were more threats to life than can be counted. I saw myself as a leaf tossed about by the storm. I firmly clutched a blunt object with my right hand and fixed my right eye upon the entrance to the enclosure.

Then, "he ho" rattled the strange accent shortly after midnight, "he's pulling it, and I won't let it go."

Turning to where the voice came from and past the sacks—only hazily visible in the faint moonlight—I noticed Fisi leaning backwards, pulling something with rare effort and agitation. The movement had returned, and he'd decided to hold onto the pipe. Someone was pulling it through the live fence.

Outside, the half-moon lit a few objects. Every bone in my freezing feet creaked as pressure rose in my chest. A sharp pain slit my throat. I looked up, and for the first time, I saw the live fence, very high and dangerously thick. Next to me, under the foliage, something rustled. I stepped back and nearly fell into the trench, full of mud and persistently croaking frogs. If only I caught him, I thought, I would wring him and cast him in the public pool, stir the water till my head spun. I would then finger him out like a winning slot.

Refusing to let fear take over my limbs and remembering to stay calm in the flood of horrific events, I waited patiently. Fisi's shouts had grown faint. I groped. My hands caught a torn boot. Fisi had been tugged onto the thorn fence, and "slowly, please, I need help," he wailed, millions of thorns lodged in his flesh.

"Then, you'd better get Simbauni back to the hide, or he'll go after the heartless thief," Fisi said as I bent to rescue him.

At the name, I turned. Simbauni's bedding was empty.

The old Fisi, having been rescued, renewed his threats. "He can't pull me like a small boy."

"This is interesting. How can Simbauni launch an attack alone?" I groped and found a matchbox near his pillow. I struck a match, then another. We looked up and down the hide, turning everything to ensure he wasn't hiding.

At the parking lot, our three boys had taken cover under the pick-up, and they scampered when they heard the footsteps. "Ehe," I quickened my pace, Fisi tagging along. "Anyone seen Simbauni?" I asked in a whisper, for we needed to find him before we pursued Fisi's assailant.

As I searched the barn, I thought of the days we'd worked together and his all-the-season encouragement: "You aren't growing younger, and there's only one life; you don't know the world." Then he'd trace his origin and gloss over experiences he never believed he went through. Perhaps our life had a lifeline, and our being together as workmates had an expiration day. These might be his last days as a worker on the Peilo cabbage farm.

No one had gone down the road behind the live fence and to the venue of the tug of war. Fisi's eyes sparkled at the mention of the spot, and he immediately left, taking in no further instructions. Perhaps he hoped to find his molester there, and maybe he trusted his hands to punish the imaginary unsuccessful thief.

I went towards the dam, my mind whirling with sleep and uncountable memories. Hadn't Fisi said he'd heard something run in this direction during the scuffle?

Folding my arms across my chest tightly as if to crush the idea of never finding Simbauni alive, I slowly let my eyes glide upon the rim and settle to the middle of the twenty-metre square dam. Surely, it had been many hours, and if Simbauni, by any chance, had come this way, his lifeless body could have been spotted.

A brave wind played upon the dam, and I saw minia-ture waves running in my direction. Riding on the waves was a little bird, engaging its entire snake-like head in its presentation: pecking, preening and surveying - back, forth, and sideways. She - I had decided her sex- was all alone, enjoying the morning waters, looking for some-thing to eat maybe or a friend or an enemy to fight. Then, a stone fell a few metres in front of her, and her freedom had been dared. She, as if to bid the morning light farewell, sank.

I looked up the hill. I saw Fisi running to where I was, his left hand holding something that his right hand pointed at and his loud mouth spoke to. I didn't want to think this was one of Fisi's antics. I stood and walked towards him. He dangled a grey shoelace before my eyes.

So you can guess what is crossing my mind when I tell you I never did find Simbauni. Our farm manager, a young man of about forty - not believing our word - did his confirm-before-you-talk trip around the farm. Of course, we had to do what he always detested; inform the police. But now the matter was too delicate, too urgent and too controversial. Fisi and I recorded a statement and were released on the manager's promise that we were to give more reliable information.

A month passed, and on an evening, two men walked into the manager's office. It seemed Simbauni just wasn't, they said, adding that there was no record of him ever living in Makutano village. And the chief who claimed he'd known him since his youthful days said he'd never heard of him. Even his phone number was phoney, and the Google account had Simbauni as a defunct betting company with offices in some remote country.

We stood from an old seat, each one of us vying to be the first to volunteer an answer. "Okay, easy," the national intelligence officer started, levelling us with his open palms. "You two are the only ones who know him. Well, please describe him."

We looked at each other, Fisi appearing for the first time, older. I ventured, "Well, he had something like a loose belly." The officer's face clouded.

SIX

The Broken Stool

When he had turned upon his armchair, the one he'd made so carefully, Namiinda felt again a stronger need to make the stool, the one that hazily stood and turned and twisted in his mind. Each of its smooth round legs framed the calf and shin of the leg of a well-fed girl; its shiny top had a round shape and was slightly dug out, forming a shallow hole.

Every day for several weeks now, the woodcarver had turned and polished his image, obliterated and hemmed in by different thoughts that stormed and clouded his mind.

He was old. The veins on his muscular hands stuck out nakedly, the time-worn skin holding them back in a resilient protest made futile by each passing day. He let his mind play as he sat outside his workshop, for he'd been paralysed from hip down.

This particular object had always been there, innocent

and magnificent, faint grains running down to its oily legs. There was something special about it: a royal quality, a healing power, yet he could hardly explain the source or path of the nagging feeling.

Many years had snailed past since he'd felt the longing to carve, to run his fingers on the emerging grooves and curves of wood and to smell it as he chiselled away, with the keenness of one on a mission.

After the happenings on that cloudy Sunday, he'd put away his pieces of wood, chisel and all other tools and had never carved again.

His father had been born to a rejected woman, and when he came of age, he was urged to run away, with his mother following, always pleading and praying. Finally, he'd for a moment settled between rivers with his two sons until the gloomy Sunday. The sculptor's objects had something of his past, and so did the words of his younger son. He knew their lineage and was proud.

The carver had been roasting corn in his mother's kitchen when his only brother had rushed in, knocking him off his stool and picking his corn. He'd grabbed his brother's shirt and flung him to the wall. The victim, seething in anger, had turned, stooped and quickly gathered the carver by the legs, giving him no time to decide where to fall. When he regained consciousness, they told him he'd fallen on his stool and badly injured his spine and that his father could not recover from the shock.

But even as he lay in the uneasy hospital bed, he'd heard vaguely that many of his stools had been spotted in distant places and that three young men had fought over one in a village overseas. To this, he'd opened his eyes to the excited faces around his bed. He'd slowly closed them, squeezing a teardrop that wetted his right ear. He'd not made it for them; he'd act one day.

From his hospital bed, he had to face a new reality: that he could no longer walk. The many people who knew him and who frequented the hospital were afraid that with a broken spine, Namiinda would never carve. But they were wrong. He loved his father, and he'd make something to his granny's liking just to prove that his father wasn't an embodiment of shame. His granny had been an early scholar and teacher, and he'd learnt the ways of disgrace and avoided every streak of it, even from his own family.

Once the woodcarver had resolved to carve a stool for his grandfather, he was aware of the warmth in his heart and the difficulty of embarking on this epic task. He summoned his old skill, youthful energy and patience, and he smiled as he lifted the formless wood in his unsteady hands.

Every day, setting upon his work at the same place and time, he feared that the befitting image would disappear from his mind before he fully fixed it on wood. He worried. But with great effort, he trailed it, seduced it, and bit by bit, through his fingers, it emerged before his very eyes.

During the rainy season, morning and afternoon, the wood carver struggled to render every bent, every line of his mind on the wood, but something was missing. Thrice, he started afresh, almost despairing of ever catching the details his mind told him, what his grandfather had once smiled at.

It was something about ownership that he found so difficult to capture. A figure on the helm was there, conveying the possibility of a change of ownership. He had adroitly eliminated the dark line from the figure's chest, running to the foot of the stool.

He had done all in his power and knew his grandfather was happy wherever he was. The stool stood before him, a finished piece of art, the tracings of a relic, at least in his fair estimation. It was magnificent, and assembling his tools, he smiled as he picked it, blew dust from it and placed it on his low workshop table, barely a meter away.

Outside, the wind sped past, and clouds hung low, racing past each other ominously. The rumble and the fall of sticks and leaves reluctant in the grip of wind muffled all human voices. The unwelcome out-of-the-season rain sent tremors through the sky and steady flashes into abandoned huts. Most home dwellers were away, shopping.

His face twisted as one does when stung abruptly, and his body shook as he bent over and reached for his stool. With his hand on the foot of the stool and his body in a stoop, he jerked, rustling the wood shavings upon which he sat and worked. Then, as in a dream, he saw the wall giving in and his entire hut coming down upon him.

When his devoted attendant returned from an errand and heard no usual innovative whistles and enthusiastic hums, he quickened his pace down a hazy path to the valley. There was no hut, tree, or shrub in sight; everything lay helpless within the fold of mud.

The carver's death became the topic of every conversation for many days until a village entrant inquired about the carver's whereabouts. He had never met him but actually bought his stools and sold them to the agents who traded them for foreign currencies.

An enthusiast walked him to the village arena and pointed at a stool near the podium. "I tried to paint it," he motioned as one in the grip of a fierce self-criticism, "but I don't know if I did it as he would have wanted." His eyes glistened.

The entrant surveyed the stool, lifting it and bringing it closer to his eyes as he altered his posture like a true barter trader.

"I had met his grandfather on one of the days," he said. "That looks exactly like one of the stools he loved so much. I swear, had he been here, he would never have sold that one."

SEVEN

The Swindler

It was just after dawn, and as was usual on Thursday, the local radio station was teeming with activity. The microphones blinked, and the phones vibrated to the rhythm of the many messages streaming in via Twitter and Facebook; the early risers were vying fruitlessly to reach the host, their voices sleepy, grammar broken, and words loaned and abbreviated.

One man appeared unaffected by the many unproductive attempts at calling in. This was his opportunity to be heard, to be felt. He lay on his budding tummy on a yielding spring bed, and his somewhat oblique naked body was hairy but oily against the unsteady light from a tin lamp. He could hear the host clearly, her voice rising unforgivingly above the melodious and incessant dial tone from his heart-shaped pink-coloured mobile phone: the only means to the hidden things in an increasingly mean and intangible world.

He often tried to phone in, although he had never been successful. Thursday was his preferred day, for on Thursdays, many callers aired one fitting event, evidence of divine intervention. He longed to be one of the countless testimony-givers; the many and the diverse, the better. Some people might think it odd that Mr. Sibia should find so much delight in joining the many drowsy callers. Had they known, they wouldn't have thought it weird; they would have understood. Mr Sibia was a skilled swindler.

Now, his mind had finished assessing all possible designs, their entry and exit points, and it had settled on this one. Here were countless likely victims, strangers brought together by the search for support. He was from the mountains, having fled from venomous city landlords. Presently, he found a lot of peace in the plains, in a rarely used but well-tended grass-thatched house belonging to a friend from primary school days.

He turned, showing his three-week-long greying beard and a jagged bulbous nose. His dark image on the red seasonally-daubed walls opposite, he twisted his broad face to achieve a look of utter determination and keenness. His elbow in the air and fingers around the phone with a mellow ring tone, he felt his youthful energy dash through his loin.

"Hello." The host was online, and they were both on air. He chose to be direct; these things were better taken straight away. "Our patience was rewarded, and in a strange way too." He'd forgotten to say his name. His *airtime* was a debt, *okoa*. His message was urgent, so he proceeded, unstopped.

"Mhhh," goaded the host, a middle-aged woman with a deep baritone voice.

"It has something to do with my marriage; truly, God has been gracious."

"Okay. Go on." The host was persistent.

"My wife, the daughter of a disgruntled farmer, was my 'friend's suggestion' on Facebook; her name appeared under 'people you may know.' Her English was exotic and very clean; her profile picture had colour, revealing her narrow gap, the one in the upper set of teeth."

"Ehe, that was beautiful, wasn't she? Just what God gives to people in this guild."

"Yeah, madam, yeah," he rolled and turned, his bed creaking plaintively. "And when I invited her, she responded after a few minutes and inboxed me: "Thanks 4 da add." Checking her profile, I saw that she was born in 1920. I wanted adventure, and this was it."

"Aha, he who finds a wife...."

"Our chat was short; we soon found something common: we were friends in a few days and lovers in weeks." He kicked his bedding, sliding to the edge of his tender bed. He had to lift himself onto the subservient bed forcefully. "She wanted it swift, but people talked. 'This is an internet girl, unfit for marriage.' My maternal uncle was particularly opposed. 'She must be desperate and bent on taking advantage.' I knew what I wanted—hadn't times changed? The world had no place for plain people. Life demanded some twist, some creativity, something brooding."

"Must have been a perfect match… did you ever meet?"

"Yes, at the city park. She declined my invitation to the Hilton for lunch, saying, 'Under the sun, things are beautiful.' She said again, 'Aye, your smile is loaded,' and I said, 'Aye, I sense some magic in your steps.' Her English suffered whenever she pronounced d or g; with very *Western* roots, her calves were thick and shiny. She fitted in the scheme.

"So…so you hadn't changed then? So you were still out there in the world?"

"Yeah, ma." He turned abruptly on his bed. "But we had to change shortly afterwards. One season, an affliction hung over the people, forcing the authorities to close the city for months. My friend and I were in the village. My uncle had demanded to see her in order to advise. So we had to survive in the village as husband and wife."

"Aha, God, at last…it had to happen. God's people must have a turning! And how was it then?"

"Not smooth. Gossip, rumour and sheer violence drove us into an abandoned village hut by the river bank.' He shifted his weight to the left side of his body. 'The owner, a hermit, had moved to the nearby market when floods killed his only son."

"Oh noo… that was surely the price, a moment for you to pay the price."

"Yes, dear." He gasped. His heart beat madly against his ribs. Trembling, he struggled to remain on his groaning bed and on course. "Yeah, but God knows. I could dig, and she could sell. We threw our money, time, and energy into farming on this abandoned land. I sank deeper into the village: one old shirt, a leaking roof and a pair of rough but strong hands. She entered the market with an empty stomach, barefaced, often arrogant but persuasive. We were genuine."

"Oh yeah, and did people stop talking? Did they let you in?"

"I wish they did, queen." He wiped his sweat. "But no, they still talked, especially after five years. We had no child. 'You see,' they said, 'he didn't heed our advice.' Again, they said, 'Such are older women, remodelled on Facebook, cannot conceive for him. Khayongo, for that is my wife's name, often cried whenever she was alone: 'Oh God,' she said, 'why me?' And I often went to her: 'God Knows.'"

"Oh, you stood by her! Oh, you held her in your arms!"

"And on the tenth year, our wish was granted. My wife gave birth to a baby boy. But our celebration was short-lived: We were driven out of the forsaken hut. We now live in a hut made of reeds by the roadside."

"Ooh noo… God is gracious. You're – and will always be - out of harm's way."

The call had ended abruptly. Sibia listened, despair and emptiness spreading over his entire frame, and his mind turning vacant as one who had presented a paper on some knotty subject to a high-profile audience. What he hadn't said tore his heart out. He craved for the moment gone.

Now his phone was on the pillow - the light on the screen had temporarily gone off - and Sibia waited for the outcome. Then, a light sleep toyed with his eyes. He heard something vibrate. He was sure it was his phone. With his left hand, he reached for it and quite hazily saw that someone had sent him some money. As he motioned to read the figure, something pierced him and a rare numbness spread through his thumb, then his hand. He quickly opened his eyes, and in the glimmer of the early morning sun, he saw its tail.

EIGHT

The Woman Who Never Returned

Jackson Bichenje was hit once again by this indefinable melancholy that often assailed him whenever he sat in their round hut near the ramshackle table upon which his wife usually placed her countable earthen utensils to dry as her naked back shone against the evening light. The reflection from her dark eyes as she turned to face him often made him look away. He never knew why, and he never ventured to probe.

For fifty years, he had thought about his wife in the evenings as soon as he retired and in the afternoons when the sun painted his few belongings gold. Perhaps he wouldn't have thought so passionately about her had she given him a child. Well, she hadn't, and she had occupied his mind the way freedom enters the mind of a young woman on an open-air cloth market.

But he was old now—sixty-five and counting. His inner strength flickered steadily. The veins on his neck were now numerous and knotty, and pimples on his face defied all herbal solutions. In the eye of his mind, he saw her as she rummaged the hut, tidied it, and often populated it with wares. He saw her stretching her slender right hand to pick the instrument. Jackson Bichenje was a fiddler.

She had lived with him for some years, devoted to her hut. Something magical about her drew him to her, something fresh like the smell of soil after the early autumn rain. He'd known this for the short time they'd been together, yet he could neither put it in words nor wipe it out of his mind.

For many years since they settled on a piece of land that was part of Omunjaru's large farm, he'd toyed with the memory of his wife to hear her soft voice again and to locate her in the mix of things. Everything had changed now: their piece of land had been sandwiched between numerous pieces that reflected changing ideas and skills. Yet he still felt she should be here to connect him with things and to bring life and order to his dull and often chaotic routine.

He'd worked tirelessly on Omunjaru's land and used the money he had earned to build his compound. But his earnings were still little, and Omunjaru always set new rules Bichenje felt he could not meet. One of them was that if he, Jackson, wasn't going to allow his wife to return at the end of the season, Omunjaru would not renew his contract.

Yet Omunjaru would not hear of a pay hike. He had

three times threatened to sack Jackson. To counter his master's unwelcome plan, he borrowed. He reminded himself that borrowing as much money as possible was better because a debtor cannot be sacked. A debtor needs to be kept on the job so that he can pay his debt.

After his wife's departure on that day of promise, many years ago, Jackson had resolved to construct a home for her. She'd returned to her people after a bloody fallout that started on an evening and escalated just before daybreak. The reason for this was that she wanted more space in the compound to plant her flower trees and the like, but he thought only the hut belonged to her. The compound belonged to him. So he let her go. Her behaviour had fallen out of the rules of his people.

He, Jackson, had no family roots. His family had been scattered during the slave trade, and some of his relatives had died in the Second World War. His father had unsuccessfully tried to resist the hunger of *Makhanya*. Of course, Jackson never saw his father, but those were days when one would have preferred to be content with the memory of a parent than to keep searching for one.

After many attempts at reconciliation, Jackson had to face the fact that he'd live without a wife and, indeed, any relations. As the two had separated after a heated argument, many people thought that he, Jackson, would stop the search after his wife. He'd composed many songs on his fiddle about her and had tried as much as possible to bring out not just her feminine qualities but also his anguish, for, try as he had, his wife had only made several promises and never honoured even one.

They'd met on an afternoon at the start of the rainy season, and as farmers went about planting, they sat on a pliable branch of a familiar tree, swinging and exchanging their promises. She appeared to him ready for the season and for many future seasons.

To her, Jackson was as ambitious as a hunter who goes out to set up a trap. In his eyes, she saw that he would be worthy of a big game in a trap he'd set. So, their promises would become a reality in a few days, and they'd entered a newly built hut at Omunjaru's. They'd start their new life here.

As soon as Jackson was convinced she'd come this time, he was awake to this heavy task, a task he'd taken up immediately she'd left: to keep a record of all he knew about her on his fiddle. Summoning his youthful strength, pinching, with his right hand, one end of the bow between his thumb and index finger and letting the resonator rest lightly upon his right thigh, he let the string meet the wire. He had started a familiar struggle to match tunes to his words.

All that evening, he'd struggled to capture her best mood, but something was still lacking. Jackson often got tearful whenever he played a nostalgic tune, so he stopped when he found himself veering towards one. He widely ran the fingers of his left hand on the wire from peg to bridge, looked up, and tilted his head to the left. Twice, he played, and he was twice unsuccessful.

It was the tune that would return her mood before

a great family task that proved really elusive; he wanted to play notes that would push her into action. She'd been away for long, and her house and home needed her grooming. But it was not just work; he desired vigour, the vigour with which she'd faced her hut and home fifty years ago.

***

The season had changed. It was dry and windier. All the creatures that had resisted the sun had given in to its powerful afternoon strokes. Jackson had disposed of all the trees in the compound and had nowhere to hide from the hot sun except in the mean heaves of his cold hut that he had hurriedly built for her.

He'd felt connected to her throughout their time apart. Her voice rang in his ears, and her enthusiasm was always in his mind. He'd known what she was capable of and how she went about executing just that which was set before her. Though she'd been a little diffident and at some point disobedient, indeed, time must have changed her. People don't remain the same, he reminded himself.

He'd heard the lady next door talk about his wife's coming, and he'd heard the market women whisper about her coming. He couldn't have believed them had his tailor not just stopped him and made known the new developments. His wife had become the talk of the village. He was no longer able to control what villagers said about her. He heard them and followed their word as a flag in the wind.

Now Jackson was sure he'd done all he could. In his mind, the tune – her tune – ran clearly as the chirp of a woodpecker. The picture of her coming decorated his mind, and songs of jubilation from villagers accompanying her were misting his mind. He'd pushed all the old furniture - remnants from Omunjaru's living room - to a corner, and in their place, he'd neatly displayed the seats he'd obtained on loan from China. She'd arrive in a style never experienced in about sixty years.

He stood in the middle of his round hut, surveying it, checking that things were in order. Cold sweat lined his armpits, and he shivered. He wiped his forehead with the back of his left hand and then reclined on his wooden table, for he felt weak.

Sounds of her coming drummed in his ears, and the fear that he'd lose the tune made his heart beat wildly against his ribs. His head was in a whirlpool. His eyes started to cloud as he saw trembling images of his wife.

He saw that she had grown fat and round. Her oval face was menacing, and her masculine shoulder muscles twitched wildly. She was ready for a fight. Was it because he was knee-deep in debt? Was he responsible for what Omunjaru had done?

In his mind, he saw many things flying like waste papers in the wind. In his mind, raced many things: the new master, land, the hut, the compound…. How could she face the fact that now they'd be under a new landowner?

NINE

Not For Quitters

For many years, we didn't know his name. We all just called him Glass due to his way of sizing up any amount of money with, "That's equal to a glass." We all knew his kind of glass, and he'd get so incensed whenever any of us—in jest—wanted his explanation.

Glass had this strange way of gathering us to his evening meetings. I have no idea how he did it. Even most of us who considered school council meetings useless drifted to his meetings and wouldn't break away till dusk. At dusk, the married among us would excuse themselves. The rest of us would listen to Glass till midnight.

Glass was one of these men who seemed to have no interest in women, which could help us understand his topic of conversation. Had he a wife and kids, he wouldn't perhaps be so obsessed with this increasingly dangerous and nebulous topic of bribery. He wouldn't be riding on the wave of high-deal, high-bribe schemes, and no well-bred woman would allow her family to teeter on the edge of suspicion and imminent destruction due to the many schemes he hatched.

Several people—I suppose in any nation—consider it a kind of sport to be one up on the unsuspecting other. In ours, where bribery has a way of stultifying the steady strides of anyone seeking a public position, you are faced with public ridicule, and your lineage must carry this title wherever they go and whenever they ask the public for the favour of leadership. Some people preferred to take the unusual path, and Glass seemed to know all of them personally.

He knew a man whose brother was in some shady place and had sent him to deliver some unmentionable goods to some obscure, well-paying market. The messenger had to force a thousand shillings note into a cigarette shape for him to pass through the control point. Glass knew of those schoolboys who, shortly before exams, had to whisper hefty pledges into people's ears to be allowed to carry some papers with coded writings. He even knew a lady who, despite carrying a small suitcase labelled 'personal effects', had to drop some small brown envelope to be allowed to reach her unspecified market.

We all knew these tricks, and you would wonder why we had to still put up with Glass for long. I assure you that he would have lost us as his audience if he hadn't kept putting up outrageous cases. Soon and quickly, most people were referring to him as *wanakhamuna*.

He had this hook-shaped nose, which would have

been sympathetic if one hadn't considered its movement whenever Glass yarned his *ad nauseums*. After he'd gulped down a glass of local brew, he'd say, sniffing and lowering his voice, "*Ta*, I know where it happened. Mano, *nono*, that's the place." Or across the flooding river on a makeshift boat, or through a roundabout route to a familiar pub, or into the familiar places disguised as a half-wit.

The weaves and turns were endless, and we received them, half-believing, half-doubting. One or two chums were retired unsuccessful civil servants waiting for their pensions, and therefore, they felt as if they'd wasted their chances—their networks having snapped on the retirement day, anyway.

We listened to Glass, of course, feeling hopelessly aggrieved. The things he said concerned us all. We were being robbed, but he had a way of making us think we had no – and would never get – solutions. Then, there was this middle-aged man with an unmatched talent for making some of these stories appear childish. We called him Sololamare for obvious reasons. He'd wait until our mouths were wide open and eyes popped out in shock at Glass' latest account and then he'd say from the corner of his thick-lipped mouth "*basie*, how can you talk about—leave alone taking—bribe in a village like ours?"

Uncomfortable, we'd discuss transfers to Liverpool, and the story would be dropped until another day. None of us ever deflated Sololamare.

Sololamare had lately taken it upon himself to

counsel young people in our village. He said, "Eeeh, I thought that was an immoral act at the village council," and waited for us to admit we were unaware. Then this axe-headed fellow would say gently, "*basie*, you ought to know these things." We regarded him with a new respect. We wished one of us could practise some one-upmanship on this guy.

***

The death of a venerable chief in the neighbouring village took Glass from us. He was also known to be very effective at doing jobs associated with such last-respect ceremonies: splitting firewood, fetching water, cooking, digging graves, or simply sitting by the fire telling stories. It happened that I was the only one with an old phone.

"I will drop you something, a glass," Glass promised elaborately. We knew that - like an eagle - he'd come from a distance, sighted an opportunity.

For two Saturdays, we missed Glass' mirthful moments. I got busy feeding my dad's two stubborn cows and didn't have time to look at my old phone. All these days, I have been yearningly thinking of our little group. I expected to hear new stories and happenings in the village beyond ours. Having fed the busy mouths and ensured no more moo-ings, I decided to visit our local market to charge my phone.

Which is why an afternoon drizzle got me running down the street, my mind drawing labyrinths of plots of stories I would hear when Glass returned. I knew a new message would arrive once I turned my phone on. An air of importance blew around me as I thought of how I would inform our friends about Glass' coming. Thirty minutes later, standing in the wide veranda of a credit shop, I was reading Glass' message: "Not for quitters." He ended his message with Milambo, which I guess was some place name.

I stood before a team reading Glass' message as one reads from a well-guarded book to some honourable audience. I read every word twice and the last word thrice. Then, with a steady turn of my head, I surveyed each of their eyes. They were cold and without any hint. One of us had another message on his newly acquired phone. He'd died shortly after gulping a glass of a local brew sold at the deceased's compound. The onlookers suspected poisoning. His small bag was to be delivered to his friends.

Someone said, "He had it coming to him, *namwe*?" Then, I waited to hear the demeaning remarks from Sololamare as usual. There was silence. I looked around, and my eyes met Brum's. He said, "Sololamare absconded." We asked him to repeat this and he did.

Sololamare had apparently refused to share the money with his family, who descended upon him with blunt objects. He'd been bribed to clear a parcel of fake video cameras—meant to end bribery in offices—at the border point.

Brum leant forward and called the waiter. "Bring us

a cup of tea each to the memory of our brother Glass."
Then, from the side pocket to Glass' bag, he fished out
a shiny thousand shillings note. We all knew what we
were salivating at.

TEN

Make Masundaaswa

I first noticed him when I was walking into the Medicants yesterday evening. I nearly banged into him and noticed what hare-like eyes he had. Quite obviously a lame-duck type. On Friday evening the pharmacist didn't close early, so I was out again and I spotted this fellow again. He was standing by the door, his thick lips parched, greasy hands folded across his wide chest and eyes searching the neat lawn in front of the pharmacy. I gave him a toe-to-head glance as I walked past; it was a stupid place to wait for whatever it was that he was waiting.

At home, everything was in its place. I opened the fridge and then went to the food store, satisfied that everything was going according to the plan. I'd make tea earlier, with a plan to heat it up as soon as our house was full. It wasn't going to be a party—I had a feeling—where people would be calling for tea, for it was already looking sunny.

Still, I opened the milk. Not a single drop was left. I stared at it, my lips trembling in annoyance. There must be some somewhere in the fridge. I surely wasn't the type to lack something as basic as milk.

I raced through the kitchen, muttering menacingly when it became obvious that there was no more left. I'd give up serving tea. Now that the wind had pushed the dark clouds off the face of the sun, I'd serve something cold, maybe orange juice. But wait…. What if the weather changes? What if the visitors stay up late? Everything else was pretty good. I'd have to return to town again for milk.

As I got onto my bike, I did a miniature planning. I'd buy the miserable milk, and pick my shoes from the cobbler. I'd then fetch Simpson, my husband from the flour mill.

I whistled the 'world without boundaries' by our famous musician Ron as I swung this way and that way on my bike looking for the nearest electric pole to tie my bike. Here was one near the door to the post office for me to lock my bike. Oh my, here was that fellow again, walking in front of the post office this time – roughly, and with that desperate look on his ashen face; a torn piece of cloth from his dirty jacket hung ambitiously past his out-turned trouser pocket. Whatever it was that kept him in this place…. I observed him as I walked past. There was no sign of anger about him.

With each step on the asphalt street, his face

tightened into a grimace as if counting each pang of pain; pathetic and yet annoying too. If he removed some of his cloths and had a nice warm bath, his appearance would be better. He seemed passionate on accomplishing some important task in this town before returning to his people, if he indeed had relations.

What on earth was this wretched piece of a human being looking for at the heart of our town, anxious and miserable all at the same time? I wondered if it was a woman or maybe a group of his friends who had not turned up or maybe so mysterious thing that he may never find. I observed him as he walked bending forward and as he finally stood at the electric pole leaning on it his forehead lined, his hands trembling and his posture clumsy. No one could be less typical of one's idea of a modern street child.

I gasped for no apparent reason at all, then went and bought milk. With about half an hour to spare I did a bit of window shopping, checking new wares against their prices and muttering my indignation against recent price-hikes. When I looked at my watch it was half past six, so I mounted my bike and gaily started riding down the road. There was that creature again, and still in pain! His gaze avoided mine. Half of his upper lip was in a bottle that he held protectively with his right hand. If permitted, I could tell you this boy's story from start to finish.

As I rode, I tried to imagine his parents telling him - "try only to look to who you are and what you ought to be. Or at least try not to show other people what you are going through. People are mean, *make masundaaswa*. They'll try to help someone who isn't trying at all rather than someone who's trying to be like them."

And then he'd try not to show the world who he was, but every time his body weakness inadvertently showed, it would just be as horrible.

The cobbler, a miserable gray-haired village elder, seemed to have lost a can of glue, and he told me in tiny details how he'd worked on different tasks. "And for all this I got nothing," he sighed. I listened half sympathizing, half cursing. When he opened one of the polish-cans I saw closely packed as termite-wings, new 1000-shillings notes.

At the flour mill for two weeks the engine had been off, and my husband - now looking really old and pathetic - had decided to close when he saw me. 'You cannot help a man out of his problems," I thought "the next thing he'll do is marry."

"We'd walk the remaining distance back home." He said. "It won't take long." At the public field a small crowd was already forming, something I hadn't seen when I was cycling to the shops. Across the road just near the public urinary, like a shell a huge familiar jacket lay on the thickets. I would not have recognised it had it not been for the visible white line that ran from the shoulders down. Like a tongue caressing the gap of a missing tooth, my eyes searched the crowd for the owner of the jacket.

A small dais had been erected and a man in a white shirt was walking about testing gadgets. He was not the one I was looking for, so I kept looking, craning my neck, edging closer and bending forward. No one looked like the owner of the pathetic thing. By now my husband, a retired DJ, had tied my bike on a tree and was trying to find his way to the podium. After all, a DJ is just a DJ, he'd whispered before he left me to my own devices. He'd asked for my twenty minutes, and who was I to deny him time for what he liked.

A local betting company was auctioning tickets for the world cup and had put up an announcement with this at the end of a half–a-page document: anyone can try. So, investors, men and women in white, like flies on a dung-heap filed onto the town sports ground. Wearing dark glasses and smiling absently between two ladies was the convenor of the meeting.

My frantic search did not make it difficult for me to hear what the man with an awkward goatee said when the jostling, whistling and pushing stopped suddenly. He was inviting someone to the dais and he'd called out the name Baxter. I puffed with anger and was thinking of the best revenge for a man who was all over a sudden responding to a name that wasn't his, when I saw them hugging each other and exchanging smiles of familiarity. I nearly shouted when I saw him fish out a cheque of 2 million shillings from his socks – the socks I'd bought him.

As I swung my head in total incredulity, the corner

of my eye caught the cracked sole of the man in front of me before he could make his bid of 800 thousand. Many things seized and tore my mind. I wanted to shout or storm the dais and scream that the whole thing was a hoax. I wanted to hold the man with a cracked sole and inform him that I'd seen his filthy jacket. As I thought of what I'd do to Simpson, my husband, my eyes suddenly clouded and my head spun; an overwhelming fear that I was going to collapse before this honourable crowd took over and my knees caved in.

Glossary of Terms

Soda: a term used locally to refer to beverages packed in portable bottles, served cold and mostly transported in crates.

Madillu: the name of a popular Rhumba Musician from Congo.

Mabati: Swahili word for iron sheets, mostly used in roofing and fencing.

Bodaboda: a local term for the means of local transportation, including those involving the use of bicycles and motorbikes.

Okala: a type of open shoe made out of old tyres.

Masanja: dry banana leaves.

Okoa: speaking or internet browsing airtime obtained on credit.

Western: a region in Kenya bordering Uganda, mostly occupied by the Luhya and Saboat communities.

Makhanya: cane peelings, used here to refer to a period of severe hunger among the Bukusu people during which villagers were forced to chew cane peelings.

Wanakhamuna: a trickster, the squirrel.

Ta: negation in Lubukusu; used here as a term for

breaking ice.

Nono: means 'now'; sometimes used to introduce a topic of discussion.

Basie: an expression of anger in Lubukusu.

Namwe: a question word in Lubukusu; can also be used to introduce another possibility.

Make Masundaaswa: ants that are seen before termites come out.

Acknowledgment

I acknowledge Shania, Byron, Bede, and Blaise for the time they gave me while I was writing. Their occasional call for attention became pokes of encouragement as I penned away. I value the creativity I gained from my mum, Ann Nafula and my wife, Beverlyn Nanjala. Had the pen been in their fingers and a paper in front of them, I bet these writings would have been finer. I gained a great deal from the wonderful experiences in Bayreuth and our insightful discussions on footpaths, bicycle routes, parks and football fields with my brother and friend Gil Ndi Shang. Ndi Shang read and re-read these stories; I will be forever indebted for his inspiration and advice. The BIGSAS community was a family, and its little joys, sadness, and endeavours were, for me, wings upon which I built these stories. I also thank my mentor and friend, Prof Christopher Odhiambo for reading these stories and for the wonderful suggestions. Lastly, I thank my brothers and sisters.

About the Author

Credit: author

S imon W. Nganga holds a PhD in General Linguistics from the University of Bayreuth, Germany. *The
Broken Stool and Other Stories* is his first book of fiction.
He is also the author of several notable scientific publications. Nganga is widely travelled and enjoys reading
and writing fiction and nonfiction and listening to
informative music. He comes from Kitale and lectures
in the Department of Literature, Linguistics, Foreign
Languages, and Film Studies of Moi University, Kenya.

ABOUT THE PUBLISHER

Spears Books is an independent publisher dedicated to providing innovative publication strategies with emphasis on Africana stories and perspectives. As a platform for alternative voices, we prioritize the accessibility and affordability of our titles to ensure that relevant and often marginal voices are represented at the global marketplace of ideas. Our titles – poetry, fiction, narrative nonfiction, memoirs, reference, travel writing, African languages, and young people's literature – aim to bring African worldviews closer to diverse readers. Our titles are distributed in paperback and electronic formats globally by African Books Collective.

Connect with Us: Go to www.spearsbooks.org to learn about exclusive previews and read excerpts of new books, find detailed information on our titles, authors, subject area books, and special discounts.

Subscribe to our Free Newsletter: Be amongst the first to hear about our newest publications, special discount offers, news about bestsellers, author interviews, coupons and more! Subscribe to our newsletter by visiting www.spearsbooks.org

Quantity Discounts: Spears Books are available at quantity discounts for orders of ten or more copies. Contact Spears Books at orders@spearsmedia.com.

Host a Reading Group: Learn more about how to host a reading group on our website at www.spearsbooks.org